KT-872-344

Hee-haw!
Yee-haw!

C334529516

'Hee-haw! Yee-haw!'
An original concept by Katie Dale
© Katie Dale

Illustrated by Kristen Humphrey

Published by MAVERICK ARTS PUBLISHING LTD
Studio 11, City Business Centre, 6 Brighton Road,
Horsham, West Sussex, RH13 5BB
© Maverick Arts Publishing Limited August 2020
+44 (0)1403 256941

A CIP catalogue record for this book is available at the British Library.

ISBN 978-1-84886-692-8

www.maverickbooks.co.uk

This book is rated as: Turquoise Band (Guided Reading)

Hee-haw! Yee-haw!

by Katie Dale

illustrated by Kristen Humphrey

Billy wanted to be a cowboy. Clover the donkey was Billy's best friend. Every day they went on adventures together. They rounded up the chickens.

They chased runaway trains.

They even jumped over big canyons!

Whatever they did together,

they always had great fun.

But as Billy got bigger, Clover got slower.

"You're too big to ride a donkey now!"
said Billy's dad. "You need a real horse to
be a real cowboy. His name is Dash. Happy
birthday, son."

"Wow! Thanks Pop!"

Billy was thrilled. Now he could gallop and jump big hedges and go to cowboy class!

Clover was happy for Billy. But she was sad too, and a little bit worried. What if Billy didn't need her anymore?

The next day, Billy waved goodbye as he rode off to cowboy class on Dash. Clover munched her carrots sadly, waiting for Billy to come back.

She waited...

...and waited...

...and waited. But waiting was

very boring and very lonely.

Then Clover had an idea.

'I need some new friends!' she thought.

'Then I won't be lonely.'

She clip-clopped over to the chickens.

"Will you be my new friends?" she asked.

"Cluck!" said a chicken.

Clover didn't speak chicken.

Clover tried to join the chickens

in their coop...

But it was far too small.

'I need some bigger friends,' thought Clover.

Hee-haw!

So she clip-clopped out of the ranch and

went to look for some.

Soon, she passed a field full of cows.

"Will you be my new friends?" she asked a cow.

"Moo!" said the cow.

Clover didn't speak cow.

Maybe "moo" means 'yes please'!

Clover clip-clopped into the field.

But then it was time for milking.

Clover did not want to be milked!

So she clip-clopped on down the dusty road. Soon she passed a lizard.

"Will you be my new friend?" Clover asked.

The lizard didn't reply. Instead, he flicked his tongue. Clover didn't speak lizard.

Maybe flicking your tongue means 'yes please'!

Clover tried to follow the lizard.

But he ran under a rock. Clover sighed.

"No matter how far I look, I will never find a friend like Billy," she said sadly.

But when Clover turned to go home,

she could not see the road anywhere.

She was lost in the desert!

Clover was sad, and hot, and thirsty, but most of all she missed Billy.

I wish I had never left the ranch. I wish I was with Billy again, herding chickens and chasing trains...

Toot-toot!

Clover spotted a train!

"Trains go to towns!" Clover cried.

"Wait for me!"

Toot-toot!

Clover raced after the train, the wind in her mane. It was just like the adventures she had with Billy! She wished he was here too.

Then she remembered: Billy was too big to ride her now. They wouldn't have any more adventures together.

He didn't need her anymore.

Clover stopped running.

She clip-clopped sadly through the town.

Then suddenly she saw a poster:

MISSING:
CLOVER
My donkey and
best friend.
Please return to Billy.

Clover ran all the way back to the ranch.

"Clover!" cried Billy. "Thank goodness!

I was worried I'd never see you again!"

"Hee-haw!" Clover cried happily.

"I'm sorry I'm too big to ride you now," said Billy. Clover's heart sank. She was right, Billy didn't need her anymore.

"But you'll always be my best friend,

won't you?" Billy said, hugging her.

"Hee-haw!" Clover agreed happily.

Which, if you don't speak donkey,

means 'yes please'.

Quiz

1. What did Billy and Clover round up?
a) Sheep
b) Cattle
c) Chickens

2. Why couldn't Billy ride Clover anymore?
a) He was bored of her
b) He was too small to ride her
c) He was too big to ride her

3. What food did Clover munch?
a) Carrots
b) Potatoes
c) Lettuce

4. How did Clover find her way home?

a) She followed a lizard

b) She followed a train

c) She shouted for help

5. What will Clover and Billy always be?

a) Buddies

b) Enemies

c) Best friends

Turn over for answers

Book Bands for Guided Reading

The Institute of Education book banding system is a scale of colours that reflects the various levels of reading difficulty. The bands are assigned by taking into account the content, the language style, the layout and phonics. Word, phrase and sentence level work is also taken into consideration.

Maverick Early Readers are a bright, attractive range of books covering the pink to white bands. All of these books have been book banded for guided reading to the industry standard and edited by a leading educational consultant.

To view the whole Maverick Readers scheme, visit our website at
www.maverickearlyreaders.com

Or scan the QR code above to view our scheme instantly!

Quiz Answers: 1c, 2c, 3a, 4b, 5c